i

c

o

p

e

PAPER CHAMPION

SHANE JONES

WITH ILLUSTRATIONS BY
JOHN DERMOT WOODS

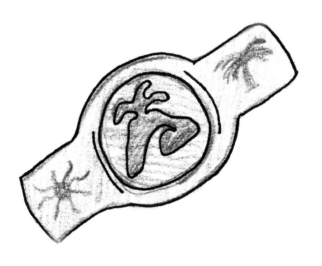

They lived underwater.

Boris stood with his wife, Stella, pointing at the base of the volcano.

The volcano made noises.

He said this was like the day the sailboats fell from the sky.

Like icebergs marching in, Stella said.

Like sharks without an appetite, said Boris.

Like the ocean depleted of salt, said Stella.

Like depressed sea dancers who only want to sleep, said Boris.

The volcano shook.

Boris squeezed Stella's hand.

A red crack zippered the volcano.

Lava swamped outward from the base of the volcano and across the ocean floor and through the underwater village where Boris and Stella dreamed nightly.

This is like the sun spraying the surface of the ocean the color of pear, said Boris.

I remember the ladders we climbed to feel light, said Stella.

The volcano stopped shaking. It was curtained by fish.

This is like an underwater volcano explosion, said Boris. Happening again.

Boris on volcano surveillance.

Boris with ocean and tears cupping his eyes.

He watched the volcano from his bedroom window.

If he was magic, he would transform into the world's largest iceberg.

As an iceberg, he would love his wife one last time.

Stella inside a puddle.

Then he'd throw himself into the volcano.

Boris, a melting hand waving goodbye to Stella in the bedroom window waving hello to him.

To fight an underwater volcano is to fight the ghost of the childhood you.

Lava runs in underwater roads you can't touch.

The only people to defeat an underwater volcano were Boris and Stella.

The Boris Books are filled with stories of intense sadness.

The Stella Books are filled with even sadder stories than the Boris Books.

But this is the story of Boris and Stella, together.

This is like snapping a volcano's neck.

Like pile-driving a shark.

The first thing, said Boris, is to try and trip the volcano by way of seaweed.

Inside their home, he lit the lanterns.

They braided seaweed into ropes until they sat inside a little circular space towered by seaweed.

This is like a seaweed closet, said Stella.

Like water burial for lobsters, said Boris.

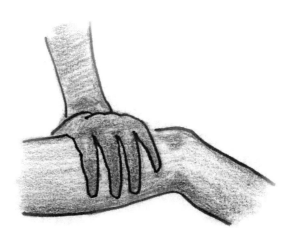

In the morning, they put the endless ropes of seaweed around the volcano's body.

At night, in bed, they waited for the volcano to fall.

But they only heard silence.

A cone of fish stretched over their house in silver.

Imagine your voice swallowing water to make a new language.

Stella ran her hand up the leg of Boris and he said no, hurts.

They forced their dreams.

Once there was a giant called Octopus.

Octopus pulled the fisherman's black nets down from the sky and caught Boris and Stella fish.

But this story isn't about Octopus.

This story belongs to Boris and Stella, forever and ever.

This story is about dancing in a jellyfish skirt no matter what your friends think.

If your friends don't like you dancing in a jellyfish skirt then they aren't your friends, said Boris.

This story is the ocean at the end of the river welcoming home the water.

Boris wants to raise the volcano above his head

    and bring it down

    and *backbreaker.*

Boris dreams lava erupting from the neck of the volcano in a fountain rush.

Boris wants lava in his mouth.

He wants to shake his hair out like a wild man in slow motion.

Boris wants Stella to kiss him behind his kneecaps.

Stella wants to say, Me first.

This is like an anchor thrown from an oil tanker, Boris said.

And the anchor falling on your head, said Stella.

Like dreaming with an open mouth, said Boris.

Like a jellyfish thinking your open mouth is a cave.

Like a nightmare bubbling with lava and you have no legs to run.

Like being alone in the ocean.

Like being alone.

Boris and Stella have as similar a lifestyle as the people who live on land.

They have orange juice because they can grow orange trees on the ocean floor.

Same with lemons and limes.

Same with all fruit.

Except watermelons.

You can't grow watermelons down here.

This story is about your shoes ballooning with lava.

This story is about falling in love with a hammerhead shark.

And you're just a minnow.

This story is about Boris and Stella smashing steel chairs against an underwater volcano.

When the bell has already rung.

Boris and Stella lit the lanterns and drank tea.

The volcano breathed its volcano's breath and drooled lava on itself.

This is like buying a sting-ray cape, said Stella.

And having it tear on a coral reef leaving the store, Boris said.

They drank their tea.

Boris trembled because the seams holding him together were anxious.

The ocean turned navy blue with night.

But the lava was neon.

The volcano shook again.

This time—hard, mean, ugly.

Lava sprayed up.

And rained down from the sky

    through the ocean ceiling

    and hit Boris and Stella's home.

Where the bathroom was.

A hole passed between them.

Little men with little man syndrome

    with orange hoses

    shot sugar water at the lava destroying the village.

The lava turned gray and held wrinkles.

One of the little men got caught up in his orange hose and couldn't move.

He had a panic attack.

He had to quit his job.

And move in with his parents.

And only talk about the past.

Boris told Stella he would find Octopus.

If anyone could defeat an underwater volcano eruption it was Octopus.

Stella nodded.

She adjusted the bracelet on her wrist.

Made of burned orange hose.

The story of Boris and Stella is like fresh crab when you expect tuna.

It's like getting a figure-four-leg-lock on a squid.

It's like winning by submission when your finisher is a choke slam.

It's like a slam dunk from the free throw line.

Nobody expects a surprise.

But we want to live forever.

Boris hadn't slept in weeks.

Boris was a hungry shark in a tank too small.

He spent hours circling the volcano, teasing it with rakes to the eyes.

And European uppercuts.

Boris and Stella waited for Octopus to arrive.

The volcano shook all day.

Lava rained down and destroyed the rest of their home.

The little men with their orange hoses gave up and swam to the surface broken with boats.

They fell in love with air, sky.

And became little men with orange hoses on a steel ship.

They have heard of islands hiding mountains below them.

They have heard of palm trees torched by children.

And everyone has heard of how Boris and Stella defeated an underwater volcano eruption.

It's like the six foot point guard going base line and dunking on the seven foot center.

Like a steel cage deathmatch with everyone bloodied and deserving of gold belts.

Octopus arrived.

Octopus said he would put the underwater volcano on his shoulders.

Stella imagined jumping from the heavens for the world's greatest closeline.

Octopus took off his gold belt and hung it over a pink coral reef.

He asked about the underwater volcano.

Boris and Stella pointed to the neon red lava in the distance, the black mass.

Octopus left for two hours.

He came back bloodied, holding his left arm across his body, and limping.

It's like a dropkick that keeps missing, he said with tears in his eyes.

Like waking up in the middle of the night, said Boris.

And being scared to live your life, finished Stella.

What, said Octopus.

Octopus tried three times to defeat the underwater volcano.

And each time he lost.

Even Stella trying to distract the volcano with a sea dance didn't work.

Even Boris throwing sand in the volcano's eyes.

Even Boris saving Octopus on multiple pin attempts.

Even Boris pulling Octopus's legs to get him out of the way of flying lava.

Even a steel chair across the lower back.

Even broken coral in a closed fist.

The ocean will drain into the head of the volcano.

That's what they dreamed.

More of nightmare, said Stella.

But this is like a trembling arm after the three count from the sleeper hold.

Like a half court shot at the buzzer.

Like reversing the Boston Crab.

Boris and Stella cried and said, Please don't leave.

Octopus walked away into the dark depths of the ocean a loser.

To see nothing as nothing.

To look back and see the volcano holding Octopus's glittering gold belt.

From their eyes silver fish pulled at their tears.

And created white nets on the ocean ceiling.

Boris and Stella bought a new home away from the volcano.

Why are there so many ladders, asked Boris.

This was a ladder factory years ago, said the salesman.

I see, said Boris.

Stella whispered that they could build a ladder that reached an island, maybe.

Boris felt something.

Like his heart was wrapped in a champion belt.

They connected the ladders.

When they thought it was high enough to reach the ocean ceiling, they lifted it up.

Too short, said Stella.

The ladder fell slowly through the ocean.

Sharks and jellyfish and schools of silver fish swam through the openings in the ladder.

The ladder took two hours to hit the ocean floor.

And when it did, giant sand clouds slowly mushroomed through the water.

Boris walked until he looked up and saw a massive shadow shaped like an egg.

It was an island.

In the distance, lava rained down.

The volcano had grown, gotten closer.

This is like being disqualified on purpose, said Stella.

Like being thrown over the top rope only to slide under the bottom rope.

I think I know what you mean, said Stella.

I hope so because I want to be a champion.

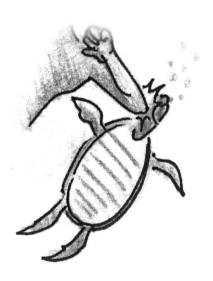

The underground village was destroyed by the raining lava.

The village was never meant to be.

Most things aren't.

This story is about Boris and Stella and the volcano.

This story isn't about a blocked shot or an ankle breaking crossover dribble.

No.

This story is a 360 one-handed jam.

This story is a flying elbow to the face of a sea turtle.

The ladder became long enough to extend to the edge of the island.

Boris and Stella climbed.

They waved goodbye to sea creatures.

This is like going to the top rope when it's too early in the match, said Stella.

It's like using your finishing move for a first move, Boris said.

It's like standing on the top rope only to get punched in the groin, said Stella.

What a sad day.

When Boris and Stella reached the island the first thing they saw was a burning palm tree.

A child in pink shorts and a camouflage jacket was lighting them all on fire.

Lava was raining down.

It came out of the ocean like flying fish.

This is like death, said Boris.

There is no "like" anymore, said Stella. It just is.

This is like getting a DDT for the second time in a match, said Boris.

Yes, it is like that, Stella said.

Watermelons grew on the island.

Boris and Stella had never seen a watermelon before.

I am the champion of watermelons, said Boris.

He raised his left leg and put his foot on the watermelon.

Then he kicked the watermelon.

And it exploded on Stella's smiling face.

The volcano was erupting.

Neon red cracks expanded.

Lava streamed through the ocean.

The ocean tried to run away but didn't have legs.

Boris and Stella lived on an island now.

This story is about them.

Boris was on the top rope, looking at the exposed head of the volcano.

My husband has dreams I can see.

He lies on his back with his mouth wide open.

The dreams form into white clouds rising from his open mouth.

The dreams are Boris flying through the air.

In an elbow drop.

In a leg drop.

In a body splash.

All of it landing on the volcano.

What if everyone was a champion of something?

Don't say it's impossible.

If Stella had the most money in the world, she would make everyone champions.

By giving them championship belts.

But that's not really earning it.

That's like winning by disqualification.

Because the other guy blew fire into your eyes.

An island is the loneliest place on earth, said Stella.

But isn't every place an island, said Boris.

The ocean was all lava.

A story can be told any way you want.

For example, this story is like a VIP pass when it isn't necessary.

Like a powerbomb after the bell rings.

Like crying in the locker room after everyone else has left.

And this story is like Boris believing he is a champion.

When he is only a man named Boris with a wife named Stella.

Boris and Stella sat on the island while the volcano erupted.

Around them, palm trees bloomed with flame from the running child.

Stella asked Boris why he thought he could defeat a volcano.

Boris said it was like Hulk Hogan lifting Andre the Giant.

Like Kevin Johnson dunking on Hakeem Olajuwon.

Like Sting reversing Rick Flair's figure-four-leg-lock.

Like John Starks going baseline on Jordan and crew.

But you're not them, said Stella. It's not like that at all.

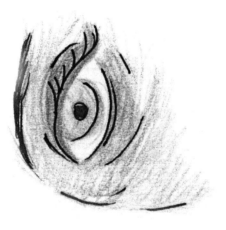

There was nothing left to eat on the island.

They couldn't sleep because lava was spraying the sky.

Lava was removing all the color, all the clouds.

I should have never dreamed of being a champion.

I thought I could defeat a volcano.

I thought Octopus was more than Octopus.

My dreams are too big for my mouth.

This story is like running outside the ring until the nineteen count and then jumping back in.

Boris walked around the island and when he came back Stella was gone.

She left a note.

The note said

   My life shouldn't have been lived.

Boris sat in the hot sand and cried.

A palm tree deflated to black ash.

The child in pink shorts and camouflage jacket shrugged, clicked his lighter.

Boris was alive with tears.

He looked at the volcano growing out of the ocean and its endless flying lava.

What it must be like to look over a crowd screaming
your name.

Imagine their sky stretched arms, the heat of them.

Screaming your name like crows.

Believing you are a champion.

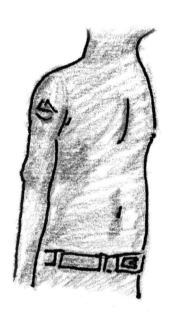

It was just the volcano and Boris.

Nothing else remained.

Boris went shirtless.

He was shockingly pale.

He had a hairy belly.

And a tattoo of Stella's first kiss on his shoulder.

He dove into the ocean.

Boris and the volcano locked arms.

The volcano was much stronger.

He pushed Boris with such force that Boris landed on the other side of the island.

Each time Boris got up, dove back into the ocean, he was pushed away.

The volcano tossed him around the ring like a skinny manager.

I'm going to be a champion for you, he kept saying.

The volcano suplexed Boris four times in a row.

Boris got in a punch or two between suplexes but they had no effect.

Boris was thrown into the rope and the volcano applied the World's Greatest Sleeper Hold.

Boris's knees began to tremble.

Boris sat down, his neck going loose.

Creatures of the ocean burned and screamed for him to get up.

His arm raised once.

It fell to his side.

His arm rose again.

It collapsed like seaweed.

From the horizon came Stella in a steel boat.

The little men with orange hoses lined the perimeter.

The steel boat crashed through waves of ocean and lava.

And towards dying Boris and the volcano.

Boris heard Stella's voice.

She yelled through a megaphone.

She said that this was like turning the World's Greatest Sleeper Hold into a Stone Cold Stunner.

Like a ten-point comeback in less than a minute.

Like reversing the sharpshooter.

Like Reggie Miller hitting three's against New York.

Like the Buffalo Bills willing a Superbowl.

I am a champion.

Boris made a fist and began pumping it.

His whole arm shook.

The volcano looked from horizon to horizon.

Boris stood up.

He elbowed the volcano twice.

He reached his arm back, the center of his forearm against the back of the volcano's neck.

Everyone readied for the reversal of the century.

The steel ship circled the backside of the volcano.

Hundreds of orange hoses shot ice water.

The little men shouted YIPPEE!

Stella put her fingers against her lips.

The volcano fell.

The lava retreated into a hole at the bottom of the ocean.

Blue water rose.

Boris felt himself falling through thick liquid.

He imagined the volcano's neck snapping back off his shoulder.

This story is like the crowd booing a foul when it was obviously a charge.

This story is Bobby Heenan holding Ultimate Warrior's leg and Ravishing Rick Rude winning.

This story is a happy ending.

Boris and Stella returned to the ocean.

This is like a heart tattooed on a baby's face, said Stella.

Like the sun saying it's depressed, said Boris.

Like you are the champion, said Stella.

Like no more volcanoes, Boris said.

Like you are my champion, said Stella.

Like, yes, I am your champion, said Boris.

Shane Jones is the author of the novels *Light Boxes*, *Daniel Fights a Hurricane*, and *Crystal Eaters*. His work has appeared online in VICE, The Believer, BOMB, Salon, Impose, The Paris Review, Hobart, Tin House, and DIAGRAM, among others. He lives in Albany New York.

OFFICIAL

CCM ◑

GET OUT OF JAIL
* VOUCHER *

- - - - - - - - - - - - - - - - - - - -

Tear this out.
Skip that social event.
It's okay.
You don't have to go if you don't want to. Pick up
the book you just bought. Open to the first page.
You'll thank us by the third paragraph.

If friends ask why you were a no-show, show them
this voucher.
You'll be fine.

- - - - - - - - - - - - - - - - - - - -

We're coping.

◑

CPSIA information can be obtained
at www.ICGtesting.com
Printed in the USA
FSOW01n1753151216
28622FS

9 781937 865344